Thanks to The Seattle Aquarium:
Bill Robertson, Tim Carpenter, Dr. Roland Anderson, and Titan.
The skate is for Cheryl.
To Diane DeNend, with whom many a slippery ripple was wrestled on the tables
of Il Bistro to get this book underway, a special thanks.
John and Whittaker, playing in the waves with you inspired this.

This is a panoramic introduction to the ocean
and is not intended to be a reference to specific biosystems.

Published in the United States in 2005 by Handprint Books
413 Sixth Avenue, Brooklyn, New York 11215
www.handprintbooks.com

Printed in China
ISBN 1-59354-079-5
2 4 6 8 10 9 7 5 3 1

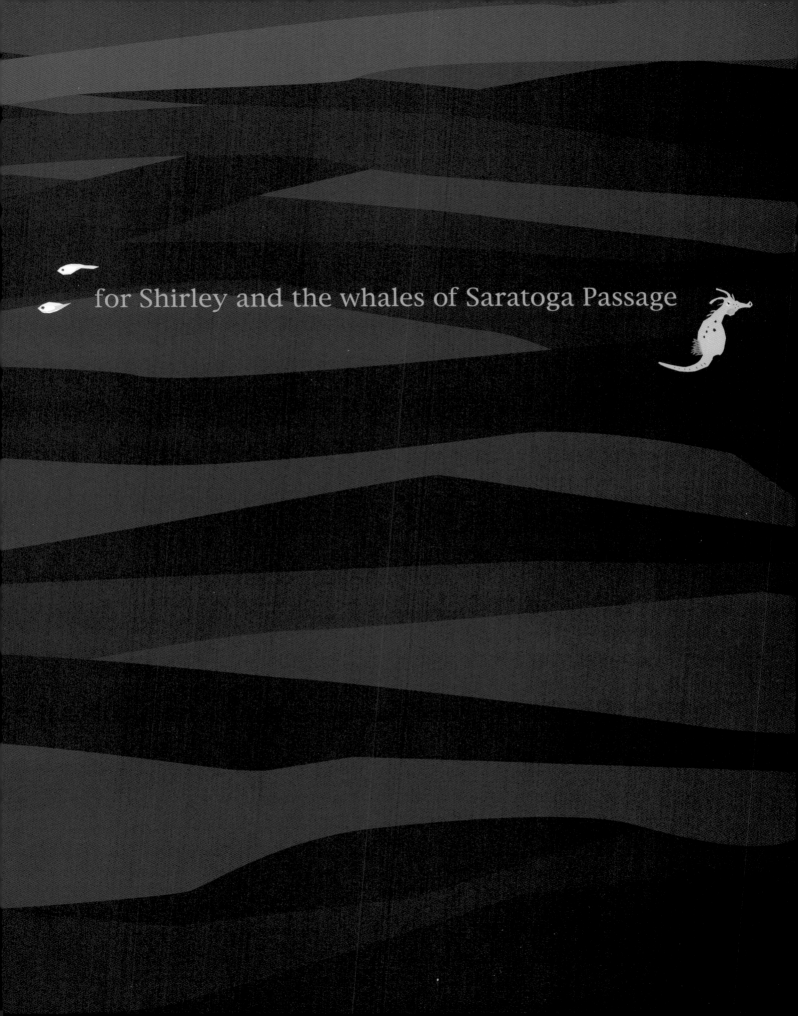

for Shirley and the whales of Saratoga Passage

Octopus
Oyster
Hermit Crab
Snail

A Poem of the Sea

written and illustrated by
Sara Anderson

Handprint Books
Brooklyn, New York

Under indigo swells
in cerulean seas

trail sparkles of   bubbles, pearl canopies.

Octopus

Oyster

Hermit Crab

Snail

Scallop

Angelfish

Anemone...

Whale

Jellyfish

Lobster

Stickleback

Seal

Barnacle

Blowfish

Pompano...

Eel

Up from the depths
comes a bubble of air.
What can you see?

Is anyone there?

Swim toward the surface
to sunlight they climb,
in carousel circles
to seawater time.

Slippery ripples
slide under the skate.
Schools of fish flurry,
a snail stops to wait.

Rolling and curling
in currents of kelp,
seals shoot through the shallows
and bark out a yelp.

With flips of the fin
a twirl and a spin,
dolphins leap from the waves,
nose out and dive in.

Crabs scurry and skitter,
clams clatter and spout.
Fish ride on the tide
and shimmy back out.

Sand and shells crackle
in briny white foam.
Beach flutter bubbles

...float away home.